I'm The Digger Driver

Vehicle drivers on a building site have a very important job.
They are in charge of the big machines that mix, dig,
and lift. Now it's your turn to be the driver!

illustrated by **David Semple**

OXFORD
UNIVERSITY PRESS

Great Clarendon Street, Oxford OX2 6DP
Oxford University Press is a department of the University of Oxford.
It furthers the University's objective of excellence in research, scholarship,
and education by publishing worldwide. Oxford is a registered trade mark of
Oxford University Press in the UK and in certain other countries

First published 2021

British Library Cataloguing in Publication Data

Data available
ISBN: 978-0-19-277772-0

1 3 5 7 9 10 8 6 4 2

Printed in China

Paper used in the production of this book is a natural,
recyclable product made from wood grown in sustainable forests.
The manufacturing process conforms to the environmental
regulations of the country of origin.

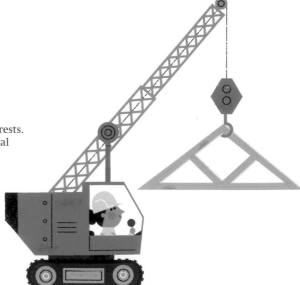

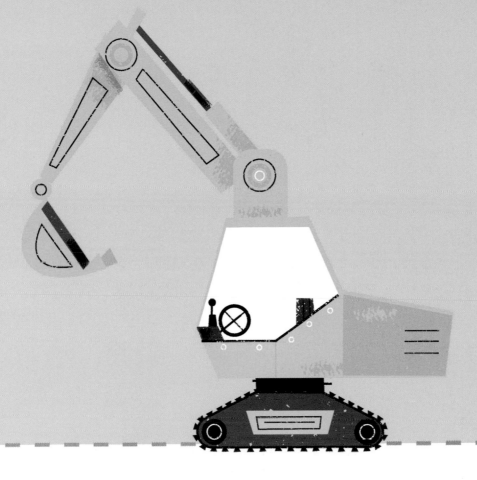

My name is

_____

**and today I'm the
digger driver!**

Today your job is to help build
a house for the family.

They can't wait to move in!

Before you start work, put on your safety gear.
What do these things do?

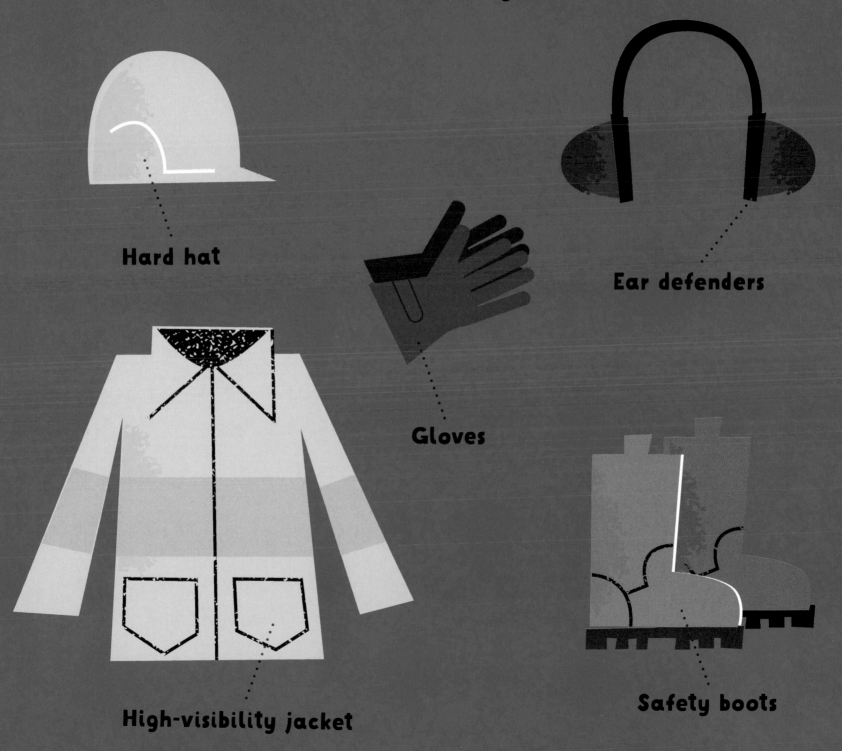

Hard hat

Ear defenders

Gloves

High-visibility jacket

Safety boots

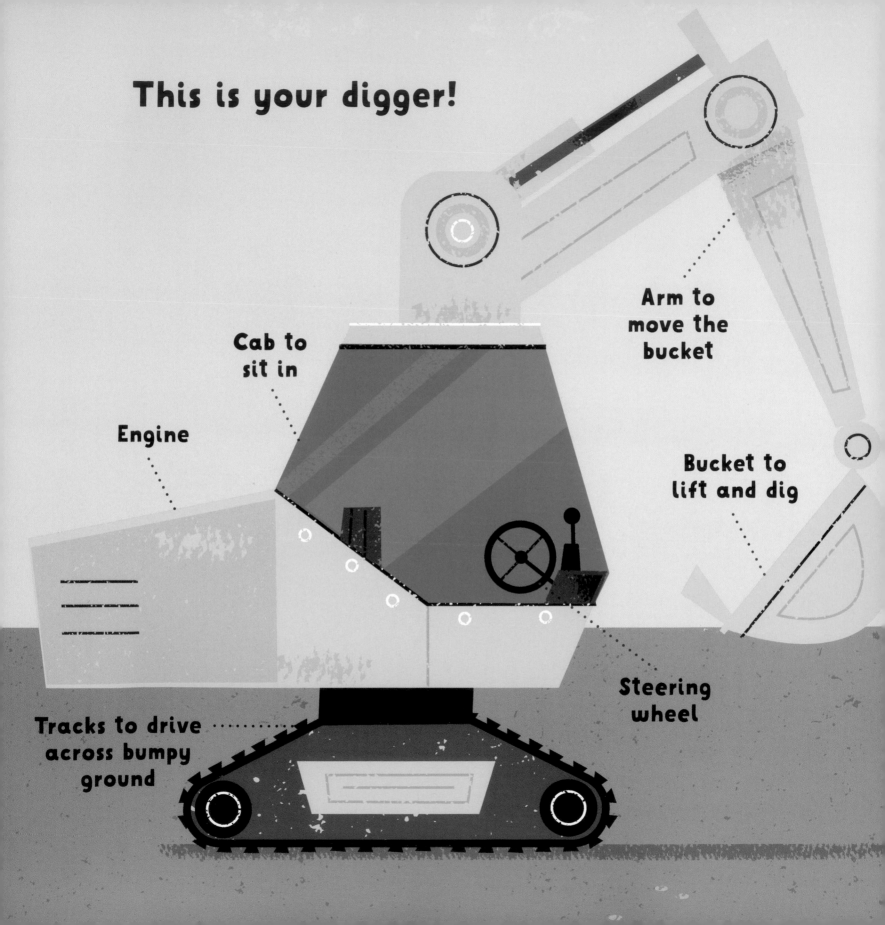

This is your digger!

Arm to move the bucket

Cab to sit in

Engine

Bucket to lift and dig

Steering wheel

Tracks to drive across bumpy ground

Your digger needs fuel to power the engine.
What colours are the pumps?
Choose a colour and fill up the tank.

Count to five. 1, 2, 3, 4, 5.
All done!

Climb into the cab. Put on your seat belt,
and check your controls are working.

press your red
button to start
the engine

press
your horn

BEEP
BEEP!

It's time to get started.

Let's go!

pull
your green
lever

check
your dials

First you need to dig a hole.
Pull the green lever to dig
the hole with the bucket.

SCOOP!

Oh no! The forklift truck is stuck!
It's carrying the bricks for the walls of the house.

You'll need sand to help build the walls.
Count five bags of sand in the store.

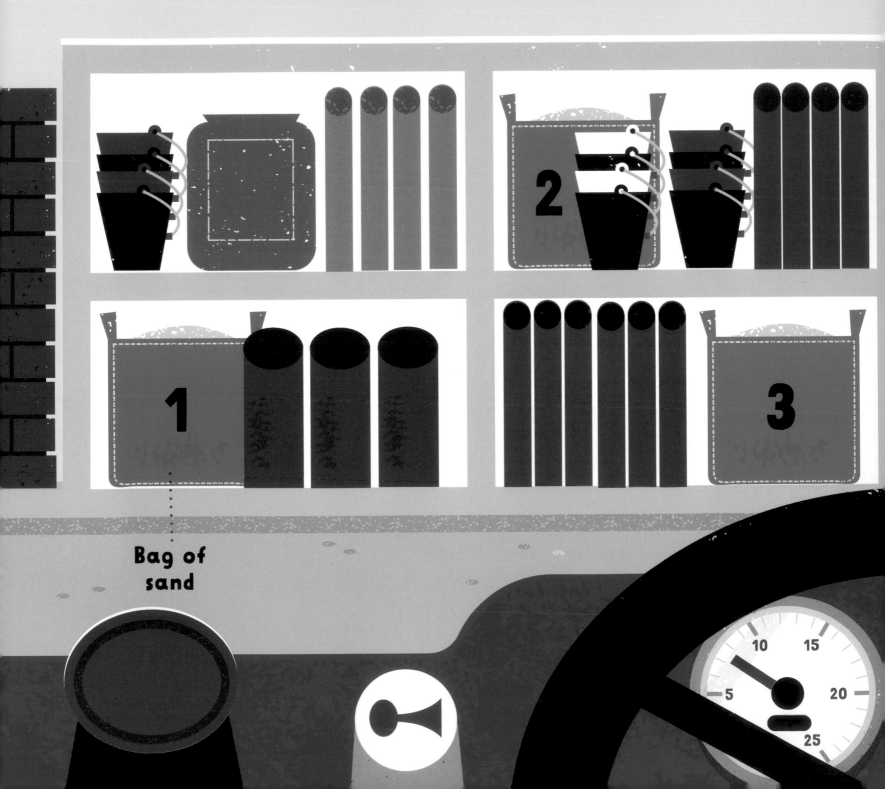

Bag of sand

1

2

3

What else can you see?
How many black buckets can you count?

Wooden
planks

Bucket

5

4

Plastic
pipes

E   F

H
C

Now the house has walls, but it needs a roof too.
Help the crane driver put the roof in place.
Tell her where to move. Shout UP or down!

BEEP
BEEP!

The white lorry is delivering windows for the house.
How many windows are on board?
What shapes are they?
Pull the lever to move the heavy load.

It's time to tidy up! The yellow bulldozer is pushing rubble into a pile. Use your controls to help scoop it up.

Hurray, the new house is finished!

The family are happy and give a big cheer. Join in and beep your horn to say well done to your team.

There's just one job left to do.
Can you guess what it is?

SPLAT!

SPLASH!

SPLATTER!

WHOOSH!